LOGAN AND THE MAGIC FISH

By Otto Scamfer

FOR MY SON

LOGAN AND THE MAGIC FISH

By Otto Scamfer

PULSAR
PRODUCTS &
PUBLISHING

On a crisp autumn morning in the Pacific Northwest, a young boy named Logan headed out on his last fishing trip before winter. He was ready for a fun filled day out on the clear waters of Blue Lake. Logan's feet went crunch, crunch, crunch as he tromped along the gravel path that led to his canoe.

When he reached the shore, Logan pushed his canoe out into the calm waters and jumped into the boat. Soon he was gliding atop the surface of the lake and only the slap, slap, slap of his paddle could be heard.

Once he had arrived at his favorite fishing spot, Logan stopped paddling. He cast his line into the water and patiently waited for a bite.

Logan really didn't care if he caught a fish or not and often when he did, he would let it go. He mostly enjoyed the peaceful calm of being out on the water.

Suddenly, Logan's pole began to twitch and he felt a nibble, nibble, nibble.

Logan yanked on his pole and reeled in his line. "Awesome!" he yelled as he stared into the glaring blue eyes of a huge orange fish.

Unexpectedly, in a deep rich bubbling voice, the creature spoke. "And what, may I ask, is so awesome?"

Logan tumbled backward and nearly fell out of his canoe. He had never seen a fish that could talk.

The great fish began to wriggle, wriggle, wriggle, so Logan grabbed the line firmly and held the creature up in front of his face.

"Would you be so kind as to remove this hook from my mouth?" asked the fish.

Logan quickly removed the hook from the animal's mouth, but he did not let go of him. "I've never caught a fish that could talk before," he said.

"Well," said the fish, "that's because you've never caught me before. I'm a magic fish!"

"A magic fish?" asked Logan. "What kind of magic can you do?"

"If you let me go," replied the strange creature, "I'll grant you three wishes, but please do hurry! I'm not use to being out of the water for so long!"

Logan thought for a moment. "There are so many things I could wish for," he said, "but I should not waste them on small things."

"I urge you again to please hurry," said the magic fish. "I'm becoming rather light-headed."

"Okay," said Logan, "I wish to be rich."

"That's one," replied the fish.

"Next," continued Logan, "I wish to be popular, very popular."

"That's two."

"And finally," said Logan, "I wish to be the happiest boy in the world!"

"That's three!" gasped the great orange animal. "When you return home, you will find that all of your wishes have come true."

Then the magic fish began to flip, flop, flip back and forth in Logan's hands. "Now please let me go!" he cried.

"Oh, sorry," said Logan, as he leaned over and released the great fish into the lake. The creature splashed into the water and disappeared into the deep.

Logan quickly spun his canoe around and began paddling as fast as he could toward home.

When he reached the shore, Logan leaped out of his canoe. His feet went splish, splash, splish as he pulled the boat up and onto the grassy bank. Then he began hiking up the long winding path toward his home.

Logan couldn't wait to find out how rich and popular he was now. He wasn't at all worried about his third wish, for it had already come true. He was the happiest boy in the world at that moment.

Logan's mother cheerfully greeted him when he entered the kitchen. Then she said, "Jordan just called and he'd like to play later. Oh, and Jack stopped by earlier to see if you could go to a movie."

"I'll call them both later," replied Logan. Nothing has changed, he thought. Maybe there's some treasure in my room.

As Logan walked to his bedroom, he met his dad in the hallway. "Hi son! I just picked up the mail. It looks like you received an invitation to a Halloween party from Kristen and Anna."

"Thanks dad," replied Logan in a hasty manner. Then he took the letter from his father and continued down the hallway to his bedroom.

"Hmm," said Logan's dad to himself, "he didn't seem very excited about that news."

When Logan entered his room, he instantly began looking for treasure. He checked his piggy bank first. Next he checked his closet and then the drawers of his dresser. He searched under his pillow, under his bed, and everywhere he could think of, but still he found no treasure. Logan was beginning to think that the fish he had met was no magic fish at all!

Logan left his room and knock, knock, knocked on his sister's bedroom door. When she opened it, Logan asked, "Emily, have you seen any silver or gold laying around?"

"No," she replied. "Why do you ask?"

"Because a magic fish told me I was rich," said Logan. Then he turned around and walked away.

"Oh brother!" Emily muttered to herself.

Logan left his house feeling quite upset. In fact, you could say he was downright mad! He wasn't rich, he wasn't popular, and he certainly wasn't the happiest boy in the world anymore. He decided he would have a word or two with the bright orange fish.

Logan hiked down the long winding path to Blue Lake.

He hopped into his canoe and paddled out into the clear cool water.

   To Logan's surprise, the magic fish was waiting for him when he returned. "I thought you would be back soon," uttered the strange creature in his great bubbling tone.

   "Is that because you know that none of my wishes came true?" asked Logan.

   "Oh, but they have come true!" replied the fish.

   "But I found no treasure!" said Logan.

   "That is not what you wished for. You wished to be rich, and that you are! Do you go to bed hungry? Do you sleep out in the cold with no roof over your head at night?"

   "Well, no," replied Logan, "but what does that have to do with being rich?"

"You are richer than you know my dear boy. Many children in the world go to bed hungry with no cozy bed to sleep in. Some children live outdoors or in shacks where the cold makes them shiver. Many don't even go to school. So you see, you are rich, very rich indeed."

After a thoughtful moment of silence, Logan spoke. "I guess you're right," he said. "When I think about it, I am pretty rich, but what about my second wish? I really wanted to be famous."

"That is not what you wished for," replied the magic fish. "You wished to be very popular and that you are! You have lots of friends and relatives who love you and like to spend time with you. Just today, Jordan called you and Jack stopped by your house. You also received an invitation to a Halloween party from Kristen and Anna. So you see, you are popular, very popular! Besides, being famous is not always as fun as you might think. It can often be quite a bother!"

Suddenly, the great orange fish leaped out of the water, flew through the air, and landed in the canoe. Logan was a bit startled by this and he nearly fell overboard. "What are you doing?" he asked the creature.

"I thought I'd join you in your boat. I don't get a view from above the water very often and I should say that I find it quite enjoyable, especially when I haven't been dragged up here by a hook in my mouth! Is that alright with you?"

"Sure," replied Logan, "but wont you become short of breath and light-headed when you're out of the water?"

"Oh, I'm quite fine if I'm only out for a minute or two," the fish answered. "Now where were we?"

"Well," said Logan, "I was going to ask you about my third wish. I wished to be the happiest boy in the world, but I don't feel very happy right now."

"Oh, but you are as happy as any boy can be," said the fish. "To enjoy happiness, you need to have some sad and melancholy moments in your life, otherwise you'd have nothing to compare happiness against. If you were happy all of the time, life would become boring and predictable. Then, how could you be happy anymore?"

"Huh?" replied Logan, appearing confused, "I'm not sure you make any sense."

"You may not understand," said the fish, "but someday you will. For now, just be thankful for all that you have. Now I must go!"

Then the large orange creature hurled himself out of the canoe and dove into the lake leaving behind a shower of water. Logan waved goodbye and the last thing he ever saw of the magic fish was its great tail going splish, splash, splish as it pushed the strange creature down into the deep dark depths of Blue Lake.

Logan turned his canoe toward home and felt a bit puzzled. He really wasn't certain that his wishes had come true. In fact, he wasn't sure that the fish he had met was magic at all.

Strangely, as Logan paddled home, he felt something heavy in his pocket. He stopped paddling, reached inside, and pulled out the weighted object. There, in the grasp of his fingers shone a large gold coin. Logan smiled. Maybe, he thought, just maybe that fish was magic after all.

Made in the USA
San Bernardino, CA
20 July 2015